6 AMAZING ACTION STORIES

BY A 6 YEAR OLD

The First Epic Book by

JED-ASHER CHAN

Illustrated by Jed-Asher, Elise-Grace, Cheryl & Darrell Chan

Especially for my Grandma,
who was the inspiration for this book

ISBN 978-9811187018

Cover design & book design by Darrell Chan
Illustration by Jed-Asher, Elise-Grace, Cheryl & Darrell Chan
First Colour Edition printing, September 2018

6 EPIC STORIES

1. The World's Biggest Elephant   4

2. Robot goes haywire   7

3. A Gecko transforms into Gyeko power   13

4. Crocodile vs. Hippo   19

5. The race is on   24

6. The five best friends' adventure   30

STORY 1
THE WORLD'S BIGGEST ELEPHANT

CHAPTER 1

One day, a boy named Joshua was having his afternoon nap when he heard his doorbell ringing. Thinking it was pizza delivery, he got up to open the door. To his surprise, it was... ... an elephant! Joshua was an inventor, and he made a machine that could turn things bigger or smaller. He put the elephant in and pressed a button. Hey presto! The elephant became enormous!

The elephant kept growing and growing until he touched the ceiling and the walls, and Joshua was squashed against the wall. The elephant decided to squeeze himself into the bathroom to take a bath.

Guess what? The bathtub broke!

CHAPTER 2

Joshua told his Mum and she scolded him. She said, "Joshua, why did you make a giant elephant?!". Joshua said, "Sorry Mum. I just wanted to see the world's biggest elephant!" His Mum said, "Please take the elephant OUT!"

Joshua said, "Yes Mum! But can you and Dad please help me to push him back into the machine?" Mum, Dad and Joshua pushed and pushed and pushed, but the elephant refused to go into the machine. So they decided to push him out of the door.

The elephant sat on Joshua's bicycle and it broke! Then Joshua had an idea. He took his machine and put it in front of the elephant. It ran into the machine and POOF! It became the size of a mouse!

CHAPTER 3

The elephant was so small and it kept running around inside the machine. It was like a maze inside! The mouse-sized elephant ran round and round in the maze and found another machine within the machine. It entered the machine. Joshua quickly pressed a button.

Hey presto! The elephant went back to its original size again and it burst out of the machine. Joshua said, "Bye bye elephant!" And he gave the elephant a big hug and the elephant said "Bye!" and walked towards the sunset.

The next morning, Joshua's phone rang. It was the elephant! He called Joshua to go over to his place and have pizza. They had a nice relaxing afternoon.

ROBOT GOES HAYWIRE

CHAPTER 1

There was a boy called Sonic. One afternoon, he was having a little nap and then suddenly, he thought of an idea! He decided to make a robot - a security robot.

He used some wires and plugged them together, and then he put a head on and arms and a body, and then legs, and voilà he was finished! And finally he added the sign "SECURITY" on it. Then he put it in charge of the door to his house. In case anyone came to rob the house, the robot would be able to help.

One day, a bad guy hacked into the robot's computer system. The robot started shooting canons at the house! Sonic used his favourite 20,000 drones to protect him and his house, and the drones fired at the robot. The robot got blasted by their lasers and bombed by their missiles. However, the 20,000 drones were not powerful enough as the robot had a gun.

The robot started firing at the drones. 20 by 20 the robot shot down the drones and they broke apart.

Then Sonic sent out his other drones, thousands by thousands. The thousands of drones attacked the robot. Again, they were shot down two by two. While the robot was being distracted by all this drone activity, Sonic built another robot, this time faster, stronger and bigger.

When the first robot saw the second, they started battling. The second robot was called FSB (this stood for Faster, Stronger and Bigger). The robots took out their guns and FSB shot the weakest part of the first robot - its chest. Sonic had deliberately built this robot with a weakness which only he knew, in case any bad guys hacked into it.

The first robot fell and tumbled and tumbled for a long time until it reached a crooked, wooden bridge. It rolled and rolled until it reached the middle of the bridge where there was a loose plank. The robot fell through the bridge into the river below. FSB (and Sonic) had won! That afternoon, they were so exhausted that they collapsed.

FSB wanted to stay in another house because he wanted to be by himself. He decided to leave Sonic but promised to call Sonic over for a celebration. FSB set off into the sunset and waved goodbye to Sonic.

The next day, FSB called Sonic over for the promised celebration. They had a nice relaxing afternoon.

A GECKO TRANSFORMS INTO GYEKO POWER

A GECKO TRANSFORMS INTO GYEKO POWER

CHAPTER 1

Gyeko was a gecko who lived in a mouse hole somewhere in the United States. One day, he ran off and got lost in the city. He saw a science lab in a building in the city and excitedly he went in. While exploring in the lab, he accidentally fell into a radioactive science machine.

This caused him to become a shapeshifter such that he could change himself into any form, like a human, a swimming pool, a barbeque pit, or basically anything he wanted!

At the same time, he also developed special powers from the radiation. He had the power of invisibility, flash speed, super grip and super strength and the ability to shrink and grow at will.

The first thing he did was to change himself into a boy, because it had always been his dream to be a superhero. He made himself a green costume with a blue logo on the chest in the form of a gecko. It had a red cape and fire rockets from his boots which could blast him around wherever he wanted to go. The boots were yellow. His superhero name was……GYEKO POWER!

Gyeko went home and to his dismay, he could no longer fit into the mouse hole when he was in boy form. So he went to sit on the sofa of the house with the mouse hole, while activating his invisibility power so that no one in the house could see him.

He cheekily turned on the TV using the remote. The family living in the house were terrified and thought it was a ghost! Just as the father was about to turn off the TV, Gyeko managed to catch a bit of the news. It was about a crook stealing a very important secret book from the government of the United States. Gyeko knew he had to stop the crook.

He used his lizard grip to climb up the wall to the window and climbed out of the house, onto the roof. Then he saw the government building in a distance. He used his super flash speed to rush himself over to the government building.

Just as he arrived, the crook was making his escape. Gyeko, while under the cloak of invisibility, punched the crook in the face using his super strength. The crook was stunned because he could not see anyone punching him. Gyeko made himself visible again, and then he scared the crook by going "BOO!". He ran around the crook to make him dizzy using his super flash speed.

He then turned himself into a replica of the secret book. The crook saw it and said "Oh no! I've dropped the book!" and then he reached for it and almost picked it up, when Gyeko turned back into GYEKO POWER and punched him in the stomach. "PWAH! PWAH! PWAH!"

The cops soon arrived and Gyeko handed the crook over to the police. The crook was put in jail.

CROCODILE VS HIPPO

CHAPTER 1

There was a crocodile, the fiercest crocodile that you could imagine. One day, a hippo went to see the fiercest crocodile (FC). The hippo wanted to battle FC. Well he was Big Fat Hippo (BFH). Meanwhile, FC was getting some lunch. He was so hungry he wished he could eat some people, but he only could find his normal stuff – fish, crabs, shrimps, lobsters and cows at the riverbank. He also found an old junky boot which he spat out.

BFH arrived at the riverbank. He wanted to fight with FC because he wanted to see who was stronger and tougher. He knew he was the strongest hippo, but how would that match up against the fiercest crocodile? The creature who lost would promise to go to another land and never come back. The creature who won would rule over the whole entire land on the island and news of this would be spread far and wide. People would know and say beware of King Crocodile (KC) or Big King Hippo (BKH) depending on who won.

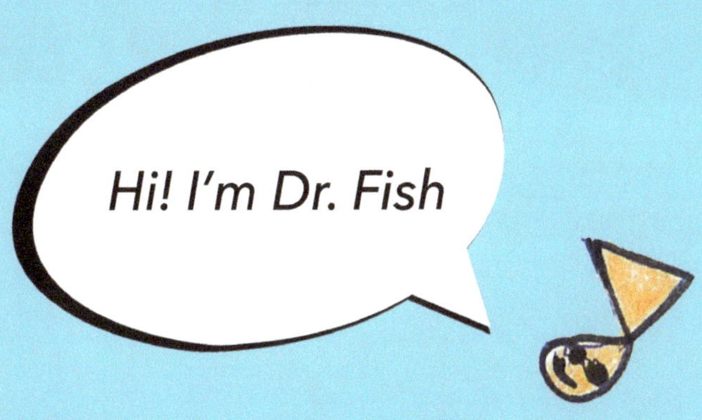

CHAPTER 2

BFH asked FC if he wanted to fight and FC said yes. They fought and fought and fought for many hours. After they fought, FC bit BFH's bottom and BFH was injured and blood was rushing out.

BFH then had to go and see Fish the Doctor who was the famous fish doctor. The fish doctor stitched BFH's bottom up. He swam back to the riverbank but because he had lost the battle, he had to go to another land and never come back.

FC became KC and ruled over the land, riverbank and ocean.
And he was the greatest king anyone could have imagined.
Nobody robbed him because he was not proud; he was humble.
He lived in a palace made of real gold and inside was a gigantic
swimming pool which stretched from the main room around
and around the palace. The swimming pool filled the whole
room. When he wanted to go out, he would swim, open the
door and go outside. There was also a giant hallway which
stretched across the whole land by the river. All the sea creatures
lived with KC in the palace.

CHAPTER 3

After becoming King, KC became a vegetarian. A vegetarian is when you only eat vegetables, you don't eat people and stuff like that. The news spread that KC had become a vegetarian and everyone watched him on TV on special occasions.

Everyone in the land loved KC and they would come to visit him, as they knew that he would no longer want to eat them.

CHAPTER 1

Once there was a peregrine falcon called Perry. He was 9 years old and he lived with his father, mother and younger brother who was 4 years old, in the African savannah. He was a nice, kind, funny and brave falcon. He had long wings and could dive downwards in the sky at 100 miles per hour. He loved to eat tiny stuff, like worms and stuff that birds eat.

There was another animal – it was a cheetah. It liked racing and it ate deer and other kinds of meat. It was called Cheetie. Cheetie was a very kind cheetah who helped people and old men. When there was a car, he would jump on the car to stop it to allow the old men to cross the road. Cheetie had a sister who was 6 years old. He was 8 years old.

Cheetie and Perry were best friends. So this is how they met: In the African savannah, when Cheetie was only 3 years old and Perry was 4, Perry was flying around to look for food. Cheetie was also looking around for food. Then they saw each other, and said: "Do you want to be best friends?" "Yes!" they both said at the same time.

CHAPTER 2

Kluck Klook Kluck Klook Kluck Klook Kluck Klook Kluck Klook.

Cheetie was coming over to see Perry and he climbed up Perry's tree. He said: "Perry, do you want to have a race?" Perry agreed. So Cheetie went down and they made an agreement that whoever wins will get the chance to pour slime on the other. The other one would have to be slimed and obey what the winner said. The winner would also have a nice palace made from trees in the jungle. All the animals would be invited to stay in the tree palace with the winner.

So who would win? Would it be Cheetie or Perry? Cheetie got into a crouching position at the start line at one of the trees, and Perry spread his wings back all ready to fly. Perry's brother was at the start line, and said, "Ready, on your marks, get set, 1, 2, 3, go!"

And the race was on!

CHAPTER 3

A peregrine falcon cannot fly as fast as a cheetah can run, but when it dives it can go at 100 miles per hour, faster than a cheetah. Cheetie said he wasn't as fast when he walked, but when he ran he got a lot of energy and went up to 99 miles per hour.

The two of them were neck to neck racing through the trees, when suddenly, they saw a tree that was so tall. Perry had to go over it and Cheetie had to go around it. Cheetie swerved in and out of the trees, and Perry flew in and out of the clouds.
The finish line hazed into view. The racers were racing on. Who was first? Was it Perry or Cheetie? Perry suddenly dived down diagonally towards the finish line…..and he won!!

Perry put slime on Cheetie and Cheetie could go into the palace but could not go into the royal throne room. The other animals of the African savannah could. The palace had many nice things for animals to do like a swimming pool for crocodiles and hippos.

CHAPTER 1

Autumn, Asher, Mr Kim, Tan Wei Meng and Smith Stan had been best friends since they were toddlers. They had met one day when they started in the same school and had liked each other so they decided to become best friends. Autumn was an adventurer, Asher was an inventor, Smith Stan was a scientist, Tan Wei Meng wrote rock and hip hop music and Mr Kim was a funny boy who always ate pizza.

One day, Autumn said to the rest, "Let's go on an adventure!" Then Smith Stan and Asher made a winter suit together, which would keep you warm when the weather was cold. When it was very cold, the suit would keep you very hot. Tan Wei Meng wrote a rock song for the trip.

This is how it went:
Teenage Mutant Ninja Turtles!
Teenage Mutant Ninja Turtles!
Teenage Mutant Ninja Turtles!
Heroes in a half shell…..
TURTLE POWER!

Mr Kim said, "Let's go to the North Pole!". Smith Stan and Asher thought that was just nice as they had finished making the winter suits.

So the boys put on their winter suits and tried to use an aeroplane that Asher had built to fly to the North Pole. For a few minutes, the aeroplane started up and flew into the air, but then it dropped to the ground. Ploopz!

The boys then had to walk to the North Pole as they had forgotten that they also had jet packs.

CHAPTER 2

First they walked in the forest. Suddenly, while they were walking, it started raining fruits because all the fruit trees had a lot of fruits. The boys took cover under a tree, but then it just dropped more apples and stuff on them. They then ran for their lives to a cave and when they got in they said, "Phew... that was close!"

They didn't know that there were ten pairs of red eyes staring at them. They finally saw the ten pairs of red eyes and they screamed as these belonged to lions!

RAAAAAAAAAAAAAAAHHHHHH! They then ran for their lives again and came across a river. Inside the river, there was a crocodile. How were they to go into the river? Asher took out a small round disk, and Smith Stan used a teeny drop of his magic potion on the disk. Asher threw the disk and it became a speed boat!

The boys got into the speed boat and zoomed off down the river. They soon came to a waterfall and they dropped over the edge. Asher pressed a button where astronaut suits appeared. He pressed another button which turned the boat back into a disk. The boys fell screaming down the waterfall like cannonballs. They activated their astronaut suits before they hit the water below. Pieuwwwwwww putt!

They started walking at the bottom of the river and saw the edge which led to the sea. Tan Wei Meng used his electric guitar and played it so loudly that it made a hole in the seawater above them, and they managed to get out of the waves and onto dry land. They went to a place where there were racing cars and they saw one red, orange, yellow, green and blue car and a ramp. They got into the car, revved the engine and sped up. They didn't know that the ramp was a super high ramp that could blast you into space. The car zoomed up the ramp, into space, and then dropped back down to the ground with a crash.

The boys got out of the car. Autumn said, "Let's go to the North Pole now." Tan Wei Meng and Autumn took out their jet packs and said, "Remember these?" Mr Kim, Asher and Smith Stan then took out their jet packs too and they all blasted off into the sunset.

Finally, at 9am, the boys reached the North Pole. They said, "Phew! What a journey!" Everyone was talking at the same time. Suddenly, they all stopped talking and stared because an arctic wolf and a polar bear were fighting. And you know who won? The arctic wolf. The polar bear decided to retreat. The arctic wolf got the prize – a fish!

Then it was soon night time again. The boys slept at 12am sharp in their winter suits to keep warm. The next morning, they found a gang of twenty burglars who were whispering to each other and planning to attack them. They took out their triple guns and sneaked up to the burglars and went Bang! Bang! Bang! And then there were only ten burglars left. The boys took all of them down in one minute.

It was time to go home. The boys found the burglars' plane and they used it to fly away and headed back home into the bright afternoon sky.